CW00797938

R S
A B

Published by BBC Books,
a division of BBC Enterprises Limited,
Woodlands, 80 Wood Lane, London W12 OTT

First published 1960 by Sampson Lowe

This edition 1992
Reprinted 1994

ISBN 0 563 36841 1

Printed in Great Britain by BPC Paulton Books Limited

NODDY GOES TO THE FAIR

BY Enid Blyton

CONTENTS

BBC BOOKS

"STOP! STOP THIS ROUNDABOUT AT ONCE!" ROARED MR PLOD

1. A WINDY MORNING

ONE very windy morning Noddy went to get his car out of its garage. As soon as he came out of his little front door, the wind pounced on him. Whooooosh!

"Don't do that, wind," said Noddy. "You nearly blew off my hat! Listen how loudly you're making my bell ring."

"Whooooosh!" said the wind again, but Noddy was holding his hat tightly this time. Jingle-jingle went his little bell!

Noddy opened his garage doors. The wind said "WHOOSH!" again, and blew them shut. BANG!

"Parp-parp," said the little car inside.

"Oh, please behave yourself, wind!" said Noddy crossly. "You nearly trapped my fingers then. Oh my goodness me, now here comes the Bumpy-Dog."

"Wuff!" said Bumpy, and was just going to jump up at little Noddy when the wind blew hard again. The Bumpy-Dog's ears were blown backwards, and he looked very peculiar indeed. He was so surprised by what was happening to his ears that he didn't even give Noddy a lick.

"You look funny, Bumpy," said Noddy. "Be careful the wind doesn't blow your ears away! Go home, now, please. I'm just going out in my car."

Noddy jumped into the driving seat—but then, just as he was driving off, the Bumpy-Dog jumped in beside him.

"Get out, Bumpy!" said Noddy, very cross. And then, oh dear, the wind rushed down again, and blew Noddy's hat *right* off! Away it went down the road at top speed.

"Oh my hat! My dear little hat! It will get

lost!" cried Noddy, and drove after it very fast indeed. The hat blew round a corner and Noddy swung his car round after it—and almost knocked over Mr Plod the policeman!

"Stop, Noddy! You're going too fast!" shouted Mr Plod. "STOP! Oh, you bad little fellow, you didn't stop! Just wait till I catch you."

"Sorry, Mr Plod. I'm after my hat," yelled Noddy, and went even faster. He sang loudly as he went.

"Oh, wind, you are blowing
My hat in the air,
Away it is going
But YOU don't care!
It's rolling and racing
And bumping along,
And here I go chasing
And singing a song!"

The jingly hat went on and on and suddenly jumped right over a hedge into a field.

"Look at that now—the wind has blown my hat into Mr Jumbo's field—and he keeps a goat there! It's a horrid goat, Bumpy. It tries to butt people and toss them over the hedge. Oh, what shall I DO?"

"LOOK OUT, BUMPY—THE GOAT IS COMING AFTER YOU!"
YELLED NODDY

Bumpy-Dog gave Noddy's ear a quick lick, and leapt out of the car. He squeezed through the hedge and into the field.

"Look out, Bumpy—the goat is coming after you. LOOK OUT!" yelled Noddy. "Oh, I hope that goat doesn't eat my hat!"

The Bumpy-Dog pounced on Noddy's hat just as the goat ran up. Bumpy growled, and the goat stopped for a moment in fright. Then he put down his head, and ran at Bumpy, meaning to butt him high in the air. But Bumpy was squeezing through the hedge once more, holding Noddy's hat in his mouth. He ran to the car, leapt in and dropped the hat on Noddy's knee.

"Oh, Bumpy! I never knew you could be so

kind and brave," said Noddy, and gave him a hug. Bumpy was so delighted that he licked Noddy's face all over, and Noddy had to get out his hanky!

"Well, Bumpy, as you've been so kind, you can ride in my car this morning," said Noddy. "And if I have any passengers, you can sit at the back."

Bumpy-Dog was very proud indeed. Goodness! To think he could ride in Noddy's car all the morning! Whatever would the other dogs say? He sat proudly beside Noddy, his ears blowing back in the wind. Then Noddy saw Miss Fluffy Cat waving her umbrella at him. He stopped, and Bumpy

jumped to the back of the car. Miss Fluffy Cat squeezed in, surprised to see Bumpy.

He was pleased to see her, and lovingly licked the back of her neck.

"If you do that again, Bumpy, I'll smack you with my umbrella," said Miss Fluffy Cat, looking so fierce that Bumpy would almost have jumped out of the car if it hadn't been going so fast. Then she turned to speak to Noddy.

"Noddy, did you know that a Fair is being held in Farmer Straw's field today?" she said. "You ought to go. You'd enjoy it."

"What's a Fair?" asked Noddy.

"Oh, it's great fun," said Miss Fluffy Cat. "There will be roundabouts to ride on, and swings and coconut shies, and donkey rides and lots of exciting things. You go, Noddy—it would be a treat for you."

"Oooh—I think I will," said Noddy. "Oh, here we are at your house, Miss Fluffy Cat. That's sixpence, please."

"There's a big poster about the Fair, just round the corner, Noddy," said Miss Fluffy Cat, as she paid Noddy. "A lovely coloured picture, showing you all the things that go on at the Fair. You go and read it."

Away she went, and Noddy hopped out of his car to go and see the brightly coloured picture of the Fair. "I'm only going round the corner, Bumpy-Dog," he said. "Stay here and look after my car for me." Noddy soon found the big coloured poster.

"So *that's* what a roundabout is like!" he said. "You get on it and it goes round and round. And look at those coconuts, standing up ready to be hit! I'm sure I could knock one down. And I *would* like to go on a swing – oh, and I really MUST ride on one of those dear little donkeys. Yes – I'll go to the Fair, and I'll take Tessie Bear too!" He ran back to the car – and oh, what a shock he had! Mr Plod the policeman was standing there, his notebook in his hand, looking very angry indeed!

2. NODDY GETS INTO TROUBLE

"HALLO, Mr Plod!" said Noddy. "What's the matter? You do look cross. And where's the Bumpy-Dog? I left him in charge of my car."

"Well, he's not here now," said Mr Plod. "And I'm afraid you're going to get into trouble, Noddy, for leaving an empty car on a dangerous corner."

"But I *didn't* leave it empty," said Noddy. "I tell you I left Bumpy in it. He must have jumped out when he saw you coming."

"You must drive your car to the police station," said Mr Plod, sternly. "I shall lock it up for a week."

"Oh NO!" said Noddy. "I want to go to the Fair. I want to take Tessie Bear. I SHAN'T let you lock up my car, Mr Plod!"

Mr Plod took firm hold of the steering-wheel. "Noddy! Do what I tell you!"

And then, dear me, the wind suddenly swept down on Noddy and Mr Plod, and away went Mr Plod's big helmet, bowling merrily along the road. Noddy held on to his own hat, and just managed to save it from being blown off, too.

"My helmet's gone!" shouted Mr Plod. "I shall catch a terrible cold. Come back, helmet!"

But the helmet took no notice. It was having a lovely time, bumping and bouncing and rolling along. This was better than sitting still on top of Mr Plod's head! Mr Plod ran after it at once.

Noddy thought he would drive off while he had a chance. "I WON'T have my dear little car locked up for a week!" he said. "And I WILL go to the Fair. Bother Mr Plod!"

So away he drove, and went all the way to Tessie Bear's. She was helping her Uncle Bear to weed the front garden, and she was very pleased to see Noddy.

"Isn't it windy?" she said. "I'm surprised your hat doesn't blow off, Noddy."

"It did," said Noddy, "and so did Mr Plod's helmet! Oh, Tessie—did you know there's a Fair in Farmer Straw's field? Roundabouts and swings, and . . ."

"Ooooh! Are you going?" said Tessie.

"Yes—and so are you!" said Noddy. "I'll take you in my little car. We'll have such fun. I'll just go off for a while to see if I can earn some more money with my car, and I'll come back at two o'clock. I'll have to be careful not to let Mr Plod see me anywhere, though! Goodbye for now, Tessie."

NODDY GAVE MRS TUBBY BEAR A LIFT TO THE STATION

Away he went, keeping a good look-out in case he saw Mr Plod. Goodness—there he was, at the end of the street—still looking for his helmet! How angry he must have been!

Little Noddy was lucky that morning. He picked up so many passengers! He took Mr Wobbly Man home with all his shopping. He gave Mrs Tubby Bear a lift to the station. He met Mrs Noah carrying two heavy baskets and took her back to the Ark with them. She was very pleased.

"Those Ark animals! They eat and eat!" she said, sitting down in Noddy's car. "I'm *always* shopping for them!"

Noddy looked into his purse at the end of the morning. Goodness—what a lot of money! Now he would be able to take Tessie Bear on the roundabouts and the swings! He could buy her some toffee. He could ride on a donkey. He could try to knock down coconuts, and perhaps take one home. How lovely!

"I feel hungry," said Noddy, as he drove home. "I think I've got an egg in my larder. I'll boil it for my dinner."

But oh dear—when Noddy drove down the road to his little House-For-One he saw someone

standing at his gate. Someone big and fat. Someone wearing a helmet. Someone with a notebook and pencil in his hand and a very big frown on his face!

"Mr Plod! It's Mr Plod!" thought poor Noddy. "He's waiting for me to come home, so that he can take my poor little car and lock it up. Oh dear! Whatever *shall* I do?"

3. OFF TO THE FAIR!

POOR Noddy! He didn't dare drive up to his house and go indoors to boil himself an egg. Mr Plod would be sure to make him drive to the police station and then his little car would be locked up all alone for a whole week!

So Noddy turned the car round quickly in the road and went the other way. Mr Plod saw him and was very cross. "Noddy! Come back! I've been waiting hours for you!" he shouted. "I want your car!" But Noddy didn't go back. He swung round the corner at top speed. The little car began to hum very sadly as it purred along.

"Oh, dear little Noddy,
Let's run right away,
And not go back home
Till the end of the day!"

"Dear me, car, you do sound scared," said Noddy. "Cheer up!" And *he* sang a little song too.

"Cheer up, little car,
And don't sound so sad,
You *shan't* be locked up,
You haven't been bad!"

After that the car felt happier, and took Noddy quickly to the shops. "I want to buy myself a sandwich, little car," said Noddy. "I daren't go home while Mr Plod is standing outside. We'll leave him there all day. Soon we'll go and call for Tessie, then we'll go off to the Fair!"

Noddy bought a ham sandwich, and took the little car to the garage for some petrol.

"There you are, Noddy," said kind Mr Sparks, who owned the garage. "How nice and clean your car is. You do look after it well."

Noddy sat in the car and ate his sandwich, and then drove up to Tessie Bear's. She was waiting at the gate for him, wearing a blue skirt and a blue hat with pink daisies round it.

"I do like your new hat, Tessie!" said Noddy, as Tessie got into the car. "It makes me think of a hat song looking at you!" And he started to sing.

"Oh, little Tessie Bear
Has such a pretty bonnet,
It looks just like a garden
With daisies growing on it!"

"Oh, Noddy—I wish I could make up songs like that," said Tessie. "One day I'll make one up about *you*. I'm so excited to be going to the Fair. I've never been to one in my life."

"Nor have I," said Noddy. "Look—we're almost at Farmer Straw's field. Can you hear that music?"

"Yes, I can – it's the roundabout music, I think," said Tessie. "Oh, quick—let's go in at the gate. I'm longing to ride on the roundabout."

"Tessie—we'll have to watch out for Mr Plod," said Noddy, suddenly remembering that the big policeman was looking for him and his little car.

"Oh—why?" asked Tessie. "Have you been doing something naughty?"

"No, I haven't," said Noddy. "I just popped out of my car to go and look at a picture of the Fair. I left the Bumpy-Dog in charge of it—but Mr Plod came along, and Bumpy ran away. Now Mr Plod wants to take my car and lock it up for a week because it was left empty on a corner. The last time I saw him, he was waiting for me outside my house."

"Oh DEAR!" said Tessie, looking all round to see if Mr Plod were anywhere about. "He doesn't know you are going to the Fair, does he?"

"Well—I believe I *did* say something about it," said Noddy. "We'll just have to keep a good look-out for him. Now, here we are at the field gate. I'll just pay to go in, and then I'll park my car with the others over in that corner."

In they went. What a lively place the Fair was!

Noddy stood looking, holding on to his blue hat, as the wind swept down on him.

"Be careful of your new bonnet, Tessie," he said. "There's *such* a wind today! Oh, look at those dear little donkeys, waiting to give people rides! And there's the roundabout going round and round. Whatever shall we do first?"

"I'd like a ride on the roundabout, please," said Tessie. "Are you sure you've got enough money for us both, Noddy?"

"Heaps," said Noddy, and opened his purse to show her. "Come along. The roundabout is just stopping."

TESSIE SAT ON THE DOG. SHE WAS JUST THE RIGHT SIZE FOR IT

It was such a lovely roundabout, with fluttering flags all round the top — and oh, what a lot of different things to ride! There was a grand horse that went up and down as well as round and round. There was an elephant who waved his trunk. There was a lion with a huge mane, and a tiger with a long tail—good gracious, you could ride almost any animal you liked on that fine roundabout!

"What would you like to ride on, Tessie?" asked Noddy. "The elephant?"

"Oh no. Something smaller, please," said Tessie. "I'm not used to riding elephants. What about that nice spotty dog?"

"Right," said Noddy, and helped Tessie up on to the roundabout platform. Tessie sat on the dog. She was just the right size for it. Noddy chose a giraffe. It had such a nice long neck for him to hold. Two teddy bears climbed on horses, and two little dolls chose a cat and a lion. Miss Monkey chose the elephant and sat on his head. She felt *very* grand.

The music began, and the roundabout started to go round, slowly at first, and then faster and faster. How everyone laughed and shouted!

"I never knew it was such fun to ride on a roundabout!" shouted Noddy. "I do wish I had one in my garden at home. Listen to my roundabout song, Tessie!

"Round and round the roundabout goes,
Singing a wonderful song,
What will you ride, a horse or a bear,
Or an elephant big and strong?
Would you like to sit on a tall giraffe,
Or a lion with a tumbling mane?
Hurry up, hurry up, take your pick,
The roundabout's starting again!

First it's slow as it starts to turn,
But soon it is spinning so fast
That we hold on tightly and laugh to see

Everything flying past!
And now it is slowing down again,
It's come—at last—to a STOP!
We're feeling giddy, so let's take hands
As down to the ground we hop!"

The roundabout slowed down as Noddy sang, and then it came to a stop. Noddy was sorry.

"I could go on and on for ever!" he said, as he jumped down to the ground. "Oh goodness me—how giddy I feel!"

"So do I," said Tessie. "I feel as if I'm still going round and round. Oh dear! Here's the Bumpy-Dog!"

Yes—there he was, scampering about all over the place, looking for Tessie and Noddy. At last he spotted them and galloped up, his big tail wagging. Then he leapt on them both, licking them lovingly. BUMP! BUMP! Down they both went. Go home, Bumpy, go home!

4. THE FAIR IS SUCH FUN!

BUMPY-DOG wouldn't go home, of course. He meant to enjoy the Fair, too. He wanted to go on the roundabout.

Noddy tried to stop him. "You'll feel too giddy!" he said. But Bumpy took no notice, and leapt on the roundabout just as it started again. Oh dear, he didn't like it at all! He soon jumped off, but he felt so giddy that he kept going round and round on the grass, his nose touching his tail! Everyone laughed at him!

"Look at the roundabout dog!" said Mr Tubby Bear. "Can I have a ride on you, Bumpy?"

Whoooosh! The wind suddenly blew again, and everyone clutched at their hats. Tessie Bear's bonnet blew off, and she gave a little scream. "My best hat! Oh dear!" But the Bumpy-Dog had stopped feeling giddy and raced off after it. He managed to catch it and bring it back to Tessie. How pleased she was!

"Here's a penny for you," she said to Bumpy. "Go and buy yourself a big bun."

Well, that seemed a very good idea to Bumpy, who was always hungry. But one bun didn't last very long. One bite and a gulp and it was gone! It was a nice bun, and Bumpy longed for another.

"You'd better chase some more hats!" said the bun-seller. "A penny a hat—a penny a bun!"

And whenever the wind blew Bumpy-Dog became very busy indeed! He chased hats all over the field, and earned a penny every time. What a lot of buns he bought!

"Come on, Noddy," said Tessie Bear, when Bumpy had gone. "Let's have a swing now!" Off they went, and Noddy paid a penny for each of them. Oh, what lovely swings, and how high they went. They made Noddy want to sing!

"Swing—swong,
Here—we go,
Up—and down,
And to—and fro!
Swing—swong,

High—in the air,
We'll bump—the clouds
All sail—ing there!
Swingity—swingity—swong!"

When Noddy was swinging high, he looked down at the fair-ground, and saw all the people there—what a lot there were! "I can see Mr Monkey—and Sally Skittle and all her children—and the Wobbly Man—and good gracious me, who's that coming in at the gate? Oh dear, I think it might be Mr Plod!"

Noddy was so worried that he almost fell off his swing. He yelled to Tessie Bear, who was on the next swing.

"Tessie—is that Mr Plod down there?"

"Oh dear – YES, IT IS!" shouted back Tessie. "Oh, Noddy—don't let's get off our swings! He's sure to catch you and take your car away."

"But we can't swing all afternoon!" said Noddy. "Oh, look—the wind's blown his helmet off! It's rolling about in the crowd."

"Bumpy-Dog's after it," cried Tessie, still swinging up and down. "Look—it's rolling over to the little donkeys—Mr Plod can't see it. There – Bumpy has caught the helmet. But Noddy – he's not taking it back to Mr Plod. What's he doing with it?"

"Goodness knows," said Noddy. "Where has he gone? I can't see him any more. Oh dear—

Mr Plod will be crosser than ever now."

"We'll have to keep out of his way," said Tessie. "Oh Noddy, he's coming over here! Let's get off our swings and go somewhere else."

So they slowed down the swings, jumped off and rushed away before Mr Plod could see them. They could hear his loud voice, though!

"WHERE'S MY HELMET? WHO'S SEEN MY HELMET?"

Tessie giggled. "Oh dear—Mr Plod looks so funny without his helmet. Noddy—he won't see your car over there with the others, will he?"

"Good gracious—I hope not!" said poor Noddy, feeling very worried. "Quick, Tessie, let's go into that crowd of people over there—I daren't let Mr Plod see me." So they ran to where a great many people were watching the little donkeys giving children rides. And would you believe it, one dear little donkey suddenly left its master and came galloping over to Noddy. It tossed its head and brayed. "Ee-aw! Ee-aw!"

"Oh, *Tessie*—it's the *Saucepan Man's* donkey!"

"OH, *TESSIE*—IT'S THE *SAUCEPAN MAN'S* DONKEY!"
SAID NODDY. "IT'S EE-AW"

said Noddy. "It's Ee-Aw. Don't you remember how he carried parcels and shopping for me when my little car was broken? Ee-Aw, I AM pleased to see you. Where's Mr Saucepan?"

Ah—there he was, wearing a saucepan for a hat as usual—and look who was with him—Big-Ears!

"Why, Noddy! I didn't know you were coming to the Fair!" said Big-Ears, giving Noddy a hug. "Hallo, little Tessie. I do like your new bonnet. Do you know my friend the Saucepan Man?"

Mr Saucepan shook hands with Tessie and Noddy. "Like a ride on my donkey?" he said.

"Oh yes, please," said Noddy, and put his hand into his pocket to take out two sixpences. But there was no money there! "I've lost all my money!" he said sadly. "There's a hole in my pocket. Oh DEAR! It must have dropped out when we were swinging.

I'll go and look for it."

But though Noddy and Tessie hunted everywhere, they couldn't find any of the money. Somebody must have picked it up. They went sadly back to the Saucepan Man.

"We've lost our money," said Noddy, very loudly because the Saucepan Man couldn't hear very well. The kettles and pans that he carried to sell made such a clinky-clanky noise that they had made him rather deaf.

Ee-Aw, the little donkey, rubbed his nose against Noddy, and snuffled gently in his ear.

"He's telling you that he wants you to have a ride for nothing," said Mr Saucepan. "Get on his back—he'll carry you both. He's very strong."

So Noddy and Tessie had a ride for nothing.

Look at them galloping round the field, holding on tightly. Be careful, Ee-Aw—don't go that way. Mr Plod might see who is on your back! Ah—he's going the other way. What's that you're singing, Noddy?

"Gallop-a-gallop,
We're off and away
On a dear little donkey,
Hip hip hurray!
All the way there,
With a clippetty-clop,
And all the way back,
Till we come to a stop!"

5. A VERY GOOD IDEA!

"THANK you for a lovely ride, Ee-Aw," said Noddy. "Big-Ears, tell Mr Saucepan we did enjoy it. I'm going to find Bumpy-Dog now and ask him if he'll give me some of the money he's getting for catching people's hats. He must be glad it's such a windy day. Hey, Bumpy-Dog! BUMPY! I want you."

Bumpy rushed up, and ran round and round Noddy and Tessie till they both felt giddy.

"Bumpy! Please give me some of your pennies," said Noddy. "I've lost mine. Where are you keeping them?"

Bumpy-Dog opened his mouth and out fell a heap of pennies! Tessie gave a little scream. "Oh! Fancy keeping them in your *mouth*, Bumpy! No wonder we haven't heard you barking lately. You were afraid of losing them!"

"He hasn't got a purse, you see," said Noddy, picking up the pennies. "Thank you, Bumpy—you go and earn some more pennies now—and don't buy any more buns—you are looking VERY fat!"

Bumpy leapt up and licked Noddy's face.

"DON'T!" said Noddy. "For goodness' sake put some more pennies into your mouth, then you won't be able to lick people. Look—there's Mrs Skittle's hat blowing away in the wind!"

Off galloped Bumpy in delight. What a lovely windy afternoon! Tessie and Noddy watched him.

"I wonder what Bumpy did with Mr Plod's helmet when he caught it?" said Noddy. "Mr Plod's head must be feeling rather cold without it!"

"Oh dear—what's the matter with the Skittle family?" said Tessie. "The little Skittle children are crying. Let's go and ask them why!" So off they went to the little Skittles.

"What's the matter?" said Noddy.

"We've spent all our money already," said one little skittle. "You see, there are so many of us that even twelve pennies don't pay for much. So we'll have to go home."

"Oh dear—I've lost all my money, or I'd give you some," said Noddy. "I've only a few pennies that the Bumpy-Dog gave me."

Then suddenly Tessie had a very good idea. She whispered into Noddy's ear and he smiled and nodded so that his bell jingled loudly.

"Listen," he said to the little Skittle children. "Tessie thinks you could set yourselves up in a row, and charge a penny a time for people to throw a ball at you and knock you down! You love being knocked over, don't you, because you're skittles?"

What excitement! The Skittles jumped up and down in joy, and then ran to tell their mother. Bumpy had just given her back her hat—but he wouldn't take any money from her because she had such a big family to look after.

"I'll borrow a ball!" said Mrs Skittle, and ran to ask a little teddy bear if he would lend her his. Then Noddy stood by the Skittles, jingled his bell loudly, and shouted, "KNOCK A SKITTLE DOWN WITH A BALL! THREE THROWS FOR A PENNY! WALK UP, WALK UP!"

And soon everyone was gathering round the Skittles, trying to knock them over with a ball. Down went one—then another—how they loved it!

"You'll soon have enough pennies to go on the roundabout!" said Noddy, and off he went with Tessie, very pleased.

6. MR PLOD'S HELMET

"TESSIE, let's go and throw some balls ourselves—at the coconut shy over there," said Noddy. "We might win a big coconut to take home. I like coconut, don't you?"

So off they went, Noddy jingling the pennies in his pocket. They came to the coconut shy—and there were the coconuts, each balanced on its little stand. In a basket nearby were big wooden balls for people to throw to try to knock the coconuts over.

Noddy and Tessie stared at the coconuts and had SUCH a surprise. One of them, a very big one, was wearing a helmet. A big blue helmet!

"Tessie—LOOK! That big coconut is wearing Mr Plod's helmet!" said Noddy. "And oh, Tessie, someone has painted Mr Plod's face on it—it's like a big head with a helmet—and it's exactly like Mr Plod! Oh, Tessie, I simply MUST knock off that helmet!"

NODDY GAVE A WOODEN BALL TO TESSIE AND KEPT ONE HIMSELF. "THROW, TESSIE!" HE SAID

"A penny, please," said the man. "It's funny how many people want to knock off that helmet. Anyone would think they didn't like Mr Plod!"

Noddy paid two pennies, and gave a wooden ball to Tessie and kept one for himself. "Throw, Tessie!" he said, and Tessie threw. She JUST

missed Mr Plod's helmet. Then Noddy threw—and would you believe it, he threw so well that his ball hit the helmeted coconut with a thud—and down it went, helmet and all!

"Oh, may I have that coconut, please, with Mr Plod's face on?" begged Noddy. "And the helmet too."

"Oh no—I can't spare that coconut face and

helmet," said the man. "They're making so much money for me. I just hope Mr Plod won't come along and want a throw too!"

"Ooooh! WOULDN'T he be angry!" said Tessie. "But Noddy must have a coconut, mustn't he?"

"Oh yes—here, have this beauty," said the man, and gave Noddy a fine coconut. He was very pleased.

Away went Noddy and Tessie again. They stopped at the toffee shop and bought some lovely toffee. Bumpy ran up and begged for some—but, oh dear, when he chewed it his teeth stuck together, and he couldn't open his mouth!

"Look—now Bumpy can't bark, or lick us!" said Noddy, pleased. "He'll have to behave himself for a little while! Cheer up, Bumpy-Dog—the toffee won't last for ever!"

"Noddy—I've some bad news for you," said Big-Ears, coming up.

"Oh dear—what is it? I hope my little car is all right!" said Noddy, in a fright.

"Well, no—it isn't," said Big-Ears. "Mr Plod spotted it among all the other cars parked in that corner of the field. And he's taken off your steering-wheel, so that you can't drive your car away. He's going to have it taken to prison for a week."

"He's not! He SHAN'T!" shouted Noddy, in a rage. "How DARE Mr Plod take off my steering-wheel? How DARE he? I'll get his helmet and stamp on it! I'll pull off all his buttons! I'll . . ."

"No, Noddy, you won't," said Big-Ears. "*You'd* go to prison too, if you were as silly as that."

"Where IS Mr Plod?" shouted Noddy, in a great temper. "I'll snatch my steering-wheel away

from him. Oh, what a thing to do, taking bits of someone's car like that! Where is he?"

"He's gone to have a ride on the roundabout," said Big-Ears. "Look—there he is. He's carrying your steering-wheel under his arm."

"I'll get it this very minute!" cried Noddy, and off he ran. But the roundabout had already started, and Mr Plod was climbing on to the elephant, which was just about big enough for him. He put the wheel on the elephant's neck.

"Nobody else is riding on the roundabout," said Noddy, in surprise. "Only Mr Plod."

"Yes—the roundabout man is giving him a special free ride all on his own," said Big-Ears. "That's why Mr Plod is looking so pleased. Not many people have a roundabout all to themselves."

Noddy stamped his foot. Tessie Bear had never seen him so angry before.

MR PLOD WAS CLIMBING ON TO THE ELEPHANT WHICH WAS JUST BIG ENOUGH FOR HIM

"My steering-wheel!" said Noddy. "How can I get it? Oh—I've got an idea!"

Then, before the others could stop him, Noddy gave Big-Ears his coconut to hold, and ran to the roundabout man. "I'll give you all the pennies I've got if you'll give Mr Plod the longest roundabout ride anyone has *ever* had!" he said. "Just as a special treat for him."

He emptied all the pennies out of his pockets, and the roundabout man stared.

"Well — if you want to give that policeman a treat, that's all right," he said. "Look, I want to go and buy some sandwiches, I'm hungry. You let your policeman friend have as long a ride as he likes — and turn this handle to the right when you want the roundabout to stop. See?"

"Yes, I see," said Noddy joyfully, and away went the roundabout man, jingling his pennies. Big-Ears stared in surprise, and Tessie gave a sudden giggle. Oh dear—poor Mr Plod was going to have a long, long ride—and how giddy he would feel. Oh, *naughty* little Noddy!

7. POOR MR PLOD!

WELL, the roundabout went round and round and round, and its music blared out loudly. At first Mr Plod enjoyed himself very much, and felt very important having a roundabout all to himself.

But soon he began to feel giddy. Noddy was making the roundabout go faster—and faster—and FASTER! Poor Mr Plod clutched at the elephant's big ears and held on for all he was worth.

"Hey! Roundabout Man—the roundabout is going too fast! Slow down! SLOW DOWN!"

But the roundabout only went faster than ever, and Mr Plod began to be afraid he would fall off the big elephant. Oh, why hadn't he chosen a nice little duck or a small pony? It was so difficult to sit properly on a big fat elephant when it was going round and round so very fast!

"STOP! STOP THIS ROUNDABOUT AT ONCE!" roared Mr Plod, and fell off the elephant, BUMP! He clutched at the elephant's leg and held on to it, feeling very giddy.

"Noddy! Are *you* working the roundabout?" cried Big-Ears. "Make it slow down!"

"All right. But I shan't stop it," said Noddy, fiercely. "I'll slow it down enough for me to go on it and talk to Mr Plod. Now don't *you* meddle with it, Big-Ears—or you either, Tessie!"

Goodness! How fierce Noddy was! He slowed down the roundabout, and then leapt on to it. He bent over Mr Plod and spoke to him.

"Give me back my steering-wheel and I'll stop the roundabout, Mr Plod!"

"No!" said poor Mr Plod, clutching the little wheel. "Oh, I do feel peculiar! If you don't stop the roundabout I'll put you in prison and your

car too." And just then the roundabout began to slow down—and at last it stopped!

Noddy was very angry. "Who stopped it?" he cried—and then he saw the roundabout man. He had seen his roundabout going at top speed, and had come running back to see what was going on!

Mr Plod crawled off the roundabout. Everything still seemed to be spinning. He stumbled and staggered—but he still held on to Noddy's steering-wheel!

"Oh, I feel like a roundabout myself!" he said.

"Noddy! You ought to be ashamed of yourself!" said Big-Ears. "Doing a thing like that to Mr Plod! Whatever will you think of next?"

"I don't know. Something even worse!" said Noddy. "I MUST have my steering-wheel back. I can't drive my car without it."

Tessie Bear suddenly went up to Mr Plod and whispered in his ear. He was sitting on the ground, groaning, still feeling giddy. He looked up at Tessie, surprised at what she said.

"What's that?" he said. "All right—if you do that for me, I'll give you Noddy's wheel!"

Noddy listened in surprise. What was all this? What was Tessie Bear up to? He watched while Tessie helped the giddy policeman on to his feet and took his arm. Big-Ears watched as well. Whatever *was* Tessie Bear doing?

"Come with me, poor Mr Plod," said Tessie, and led him away. Big-Ears and Noddy followed in astonishment. Across the big field they went, past the swings and the stalls—right over to the coconut shy.

"Gracious! He'll see his helmet on that coconut head!" said Noddy, in alarm. "Tessie—come back!"

"COME WITH ME, POOR MR PLOD," SAID TESSIE AND LED HIM AWAY

But Tessie Bear took no notice. "*I'll* give you back your helmet, poor Mr Plod," she said. "Your head will catch cold without it. But you WILL keep your promise and give me Noddy's steering-wheel in exchange, won't you?"

"Yes, Tessie, I will," said Mr Plod, not feeling so giddy now. "Where is it? Show it to me."

"There it is!" said Tessie, and pointed to the coconut with Mr Plod's face painted on it. "That big coconut is wearing it. Now give me Noddy's steering-wheel, please."

Mr Plod didn't give it to her. He was so surprised and angry to see a coconut wearing his helmet that he dropped the wheel on the ground, strode in among all the coconuts and snatched his helmet with a great roar.

"WHO PUT MY HELMET ON A COCONUT? JUST TELL ME THAT! AND WHO DREW MY FACE ON IT?"

The coconut shy man fled. So did everyone else, Noddy and Tessie too! Big-Ears raced to get his bicycle. The Saucepan Man leapt on his donkey and galloped away. The Skittles ran for their lives. Bumpy-Dog raced off, barking.

Soon there was only Mr Plod left at the Fair. Everyone had gone or was hiding. "Where's that steering-wheel?" said Mr Plod, looking all round. But it was gone, of course. Mr Plod put on his helmet and felt a little better. Now to deal with Noddy and his car!

Noddy had raced to his car with Tessie, carrying the precious steering-wheel. He had fitted it quickly into place—and jumped into the driving seat.

"Come along, Tessie!" he cried. "I've got some jam tarts and sugar biscuits at home. We'll go back to my little House-For-One and have some tea! Hurry, little car! I want to lock you safely up before Mr Plod comes looking for you!"

And away they went, with Bumpy-Dog standing at the back, wagging his tail. Noddy was so happy that he simply couldn't help singing at the top of his voice. Listen!

"Oh, now we are happy,
As happy as can be,
For we're driving home
To a wonderful tea!
Bark, little Bumpy,
Smile, Tessie Bear.
Oh, wasn't it FUN
To go to the Fair!"

It was fun, Noddy! We enjoyed it too!

THE NODDY LIBRARY

1. NODDY GOES TO TOYLAND
2. HURRAH FOR LITTLE NODDY
3. NODDY AND HIS CAR
4. HERE COMES NODDY AGAIN!
5. WELL DONE NODDY!
6. NODDY GOES TO SCHOOL
7. NODDY AT THE SEASIDE
8. NODDY GETS INTO TROUBLE
9. NODDY AND THE MAGIC RUBBER
10. YOU FUNNY LITTLE NODDY
11. NODDY MEETS FATHER CHRISTMAS
12. NODDY AND TESSIE BEAR
13. BE BRAVE LITTLE NODDY!
14. NODDY AND THE BUMPY-DOG
15. DO LOOK OUT NODDY!
16. YOU'RE A GOOD FRIEND NODDY!
17. NODDY HAS AN ADVENTURE
18. NODDY GOES TO SEA
19. NODDY AND THE BUNKEY
20. CHEER UP LITTLE NODDY!
21. NODDY GOES TO THE FAIR
22. MR PLOD AND LITTLE NODDY
23. NODDY AND THE TOOTLES
24. NODDY AND THE AEROPLANE